CW00865146

This book belongs to

_____

Bow's Background

This is a story based on our family sausage dog Bow. Bow comes from a small town in England called Loughborough. From a young age Bow has always liked to go on adventures
in some of the most 'interesting' of places, from the tightest gaps in our house to the smallest unknown passageways hidden in our garden.
She absolutely loves scavenging for food and always manages to convince the children to give her a bit of their cake!

For Arlo and Ezra

Copyright © 2022 by Sam Hinton

All rights reserved. No part of this book may be reproduced, stored or introduced into
a retrieval system, or transmitted in any form without prior written permission
of the copyright owner/publisher.

Where's Bow?

By Sam Hinton

It's time to take our doggy out, to run around and play,

But that cheeky little sausage is playing hide and seek today!

Where's Bow? Where's Bow?

Not the bin, that's way too smelly!

There's Bow! There's Bow!

She's hiding in my welly!

Into the car we go, as we drive off to the massive park,

But that cheeky doggy makes no sound,

not a growl, a lick, nor bark.

Where's Bow? Where's Bow?

I can't see her paws or nose.

There's Bow! There's Bow!

She's in our bag of clothes!

Off to the park we go, we've got Bow's stick
and her favourite ball,
But that cheeky little sausage can't be
seen anywhere at all!

Where's Bow? Where's Bow?
Let's look on the count of 3...
There's Bow! There's Bow!
She's hiding behind the tree!

Our special furry doggy sees another friend ahead,
But that cheeky little sausage starts chasing them
instead!

Where's Bow? Where's Bow?
Is she pretending to be a log?
There's Bow! There's Bow!
She's lying on that dog!

It's time to go back home and get settled with a bath,
Because that cheeky little sausage jumped in
mud straight off the path!

Where's Bow? Where's Bow?
We want to give her a cuddle.
There's Bow! There's Bow!
She's hiding in the puddle!

We're back home now from our lovely walk,

and it's time to get cleaned up,

Where is that cheeky sausage? That muddy little pup!

Where's Bow? Where's Bow?

She's made paw prints on the floor!

There's Bow! There's Bow!

She's hiding behind the door!

The bath is full of bubbles, soap and brush are at the ready,
That cheeky sausage is hiding somewhere, keeping herself steady!

Where's Bow? Where's Bow?
The water is getting colder.
There's Bow! There's Bow!
She's being a loo roll holder!

It's time to bring the towel out to get her nice and dry,
Where ever is that cheeky sausage, I'm sure she's just ran by!

Where's Bow? Where's Bow?
She's in that room, I'm certain!
There's Bow! There's Bow!
She's hiding behind the curtain!

It's time to go to bed now and dream the night away,

Bow's resting in her basket, planning

where to hide the next day!

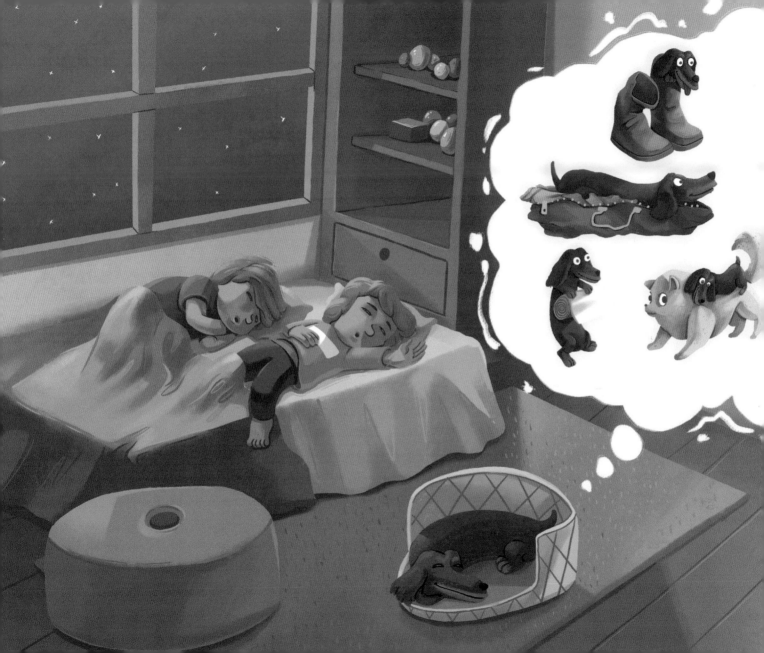

Thank you for joining us on this adventure.

I hope you enjoyed reading it

as much as I did writing it.

Bow the sausage dog will be returning...When we

eventually find out where she's been hiding!

Bow

<u>Idea</u>

The idea for the 'Where's Bow?' story came from a time when we were getting ready to go on a walk and couldn't find Bow anywhere in the house. We spent a good 20 minutes calling her name and looking under every bed, table and cupboard in the house. She was nowhere to be seen. It was only until we went upstairs for the second time that we noticed 2 small paws stood perfectly still under our bathroom door.

Bow was completely silent and not responding to any of her calls. The paws remained unmoved. When we went to open the bathroom door she was jumping around all happy and excited as if she'd realised how amazing she'd been at playing hide and seek.

This wasn't her last game.

Dachsund Detail

• Dachsunds were originally bred for their size and length to allow them to burrow in to the smallest of holes for the purpose of looking for wild badgers and rabbits underground, so naturally they are likely to be seen hiding in places similar to that, such as: behind the sofa, the arm of a jumper and even inside a wellington boot!

• Dachsunds are the smallest type of hound dog

• Dachsunds love to bark, one of the reasons why their bark is so loud is so that they can be tracked by their owner if they burrow underground.

• Dachsunds don't let their size affect their pride. You will often find a Dachsund always sticks up for itself and stands it's ground regardless of it's height and shape.

• Because of their length, you have to pick them up at both ends to keep their back supported. Similar to the way you would carry a rolled up rug.

• Some dachsunds have the ability to sit on their hind legs, with their back upright like a meerkat. This is often used as a begging pose to gain food and treats.

.Dachsunds don't get taught tricks, they simply show their owners how to give them treats.

About Bow

<u>Name:</u> Bow

<u>Weight:</u> 6kg

<u>Breed:</u> Pedigree Miniature Dachsund

<u>Hair Type:</u> Long Haired

<u>Birth Place:</u> Hertfordshire

<u>Home Town:</u> Loughborough

<u>Nicknames:</u> Bowie, Bowchops, B-dog & Bow-Bow

<u>Favourite food:</u> Cheese

<u>Favourite toy:</u> Sally the sausage dog cuddly plush

<u>Best place to nap:</u> On the top of the sofa where the sun shines

<u>Tricks:</u> Roll over, Handshake, Meerkat, High five, Patience

<u>Pet Peeves:</u> Barking at other dogs twice the size of her then running away

<u>Favourite hiding place:</u> Under the sofa

Special Thanks

A special thank you to my loving wife Chantelle,

For always keeping our family feeling happy and loved.

Printed in Great Britain
by Amazon

78381039R00018